Produced by Kroha Associates, Inc.
Middletown, Connecticut.

Illustrated by Alvin S. White Studio
Burbank, California.

Printed in the United States of America.

ISBN 1-56326-007-7

Helping Hands

Today is an exciting day for the Disney Babies.
Soon, visitors will come to see their classroom. The
Disney Babies are busy making their classroom nice
and neat.

Baby Mickey puts books back on the shelf. "All done!" says Baby Mickey. Baby Minnie dusts the crumbs off the snack table. Baby Clarabelle throws away the milk cartons. Baby Goofy puts away the toys.

All the books are lined up on the shelf. Most of
the toys are back in the toy chest. The snack table
is clean. There is just one more thing for the Disney
Babies to do.

They want to paint a beautiful picture to decorate their classroom. But there is not much time. The visitors will arrive soon. The Disney Babies must hurry!

Each Disney Baby has a job to do. If everyone helps, the picture will be done in time. Baby Goofy goes to get the paintbrushes. Baby Minnie goes to get the paints. Baby Clarabelle goes to get the paint smocks.

Baby Mickey is ahead of the others. He has already gotten the big roll of art paper from the corner. Baby Mickey is excited. He cannot wait to start work on the beautiful picture.

Baby Mickey unrolls the paper carefully. It is hard to keep it flat. The ends curl up! He holds the edges down with books.

Baby Mickey looks around. Uh-oh! The other Disney Babies are all very busy doing other things. They have forgotten all about painting the picture!

"Look!" says Baby Goofy proudly. He is making lots and lots of big bubbles. The bubbles sparkle and shine. Some tickle Baby Goofy's nose. Baby Goofy loves bubbles. He is having fun.

Baby Mickey is worried. It is getting late. The visitors will be here soon. No one is working on the beautiful picture yet! Then Baby Mickey sees the other Disney Babies.

Baby Clarabelle and Baby Minnie are playing dress up. Baby Clarabelle tries on the floppy, yellow hat and looks at herself in the mirror. "Pretty!" says Baby Clarabelle.

Baby Minnie finds a scarf made of bright pink
feathers. She wraps it around herself. "Pretty too!"
says Baby Minnie. All the Disney Babies have
forgotten about helping Baby Mickey.

Baby Mickey has an idea. He heads for the music shelf. He picks up the big, shiny cymbals.

BING! BANG! BOING! Baby Mickey clangs the cymbals together. All the Disney Babies stop playing and look at Baby Mickey in surprise! What's wrong?

"Help paint!" says Baby Mickey loudly.

Suddenly, the Disney Babies remember! They must hurry and paint the beautiful picture. Baby Goofy claps his hands and breaks the bubbles in the sink. Then he gets the paintbrushes.

Baby Clarabelle puts the floppy hat in the toy chest. Then she gets the smocks. Baby Minnie puts away the pink scarf. Then she gets the paints for the picture.

The Disney Babies work on their beautiful picture
Baby Mickey is smiling. He is painting a picture of
the Disney Babies' preschool. Baby Minnie is
painting a blue sky.

Baby Goofy is painting a yellow sun. Baby
Clarabelle is painting green trees and grass. They
must hurry to finish before the visitors arrive.

Finally, their picture is all finished. They hold it up
and look at it. It is so pretty! "Hooray! Hooray!"
cheer the Disney Babies.

The Disney Babies are proud of their work. Every Disney Baby helped to make the picture beautiful. And it is finished just in time. Here come the visitors now!

Parenting Matters

Dear Parent,

Learning to work harmoniously with others and to be responsible is an important part of growing up. Even very young children can do part of a larger task and contribute to a job that would otherwise be too complicated for them to do.

In *Helping Hands*, the *Disney Babies* have only a little time to do a big job. Visitors are coming to their preschool and the *Disney Babies* must work together to straighten up their classroom and paint a mural to greet the guests. To make the project easier, each *Disney Baby* has a clean-up task to do and a painting task to do. But, when the babies forget their assignments and play instead, it appears that the job will not get done. Then Baby Mickey reminds them of their responsibilities, and the *Disney Babies* all work together until the job is done. In the end, the welcome mural is completed just in time — and it is beautiful!

Helping Hands **helps young children learn that:**

- it is important to do their part when others are relying on them.
- big jobs can be done quickly and successfully when people work together for one purpose.
- working with others to achieve a goal is enjoyable.
- they should feel proud of their accomplishments.

Some Hints for Parents

- Give children small tasks to do along with you. Show them how to fold hand towels as you fold the laundry.
- Help children do complicated tasks by giving them step-by-step directions to follow. Don't tell them to clean their rooms. Instead, tell them to put the blocks inside the toy chest, stack the books on the shelf, and throw the dirty clothes into the laundry basket.
- Compliment children when they complete their tasks, even when the results are less than perfect.